The Cats of Laughing Thunder in

The New Businesses Adventure

S. S. Curtis

ISBN 1732329915

www.laughingthunder.com

Cast of Characters

The Four Friends

Fritz – tousled gray fur; likes meteorology and music

Pumpkin – bright orange fur; likes unmannerliness and action

Sven – brown tabby fur; likes cooking and Vikings

Yolanda – black and white tuxedo-marked fur; likes robots and science

The Adults

Ferd – gray fur; Fritz's uncle

Penrietta – orange fur; Pumpkin's grandmother

Sigrid – brown tabby fur; Sven's mother

Teacher Ms. Robo Kitty – brown and white tuxedo-marked fur; Cat School teacher

The Teens

Azola – tortoiseshell fur; president of student government; likes plants

Boris – orange-and-white-spotted fur; likes lime-flavored chips

Skoog – cream fur; likes sleep research

Yosh – black and white tuxedo-marked fur; Yolanda's older brother; likes marine life

Chapter 1

Pumpkin and his cat friends stared longingly at the candy in the window of the general store.

"Let's buy some!" said Pumpkin, swishing his bright orange tail eagerly.

Yolanda, a cat with black and white tuxedo markings, nodded her head in agreement.

"That is fudge. It has lots of yummy cream in it," said Sven. The brown tabby's mouth watered.

"But none of us has any money," said Fritz, as he raked his already tousled gray fur with his claws.

The cats turned their backs on the candy display, and dropped their heads sadly.

Yolanda straightened up. "I know!" she said.

"We each need to start a business to earn money. Then we can buy candy!"

"What kind of businesses?" asked Sven.

"Let's go home and think about it," said Yolanda.

Chapter 2

Fritz's Weather Blog

Tuesday, March 14:

Weather Forecast for Josheka Farm, Laughing Thunder County, Minnesota - Clear with a high of 44 degrees Fahrenheit

The next morning, the friends met up on their way to Cat School.

"Uncle Ferd paid me this month's allowance, and gave me a birthday gift of money. I used all of that money to buy a small weather blimp," said Fritz.

"By the Great Cat!" said Yolanda. "What are you going to do with that?"

"My business is going to be a weather blog.

I'll shoot video from the blimp," said Fritz. "What about the rest of you?"

"I am going to do a cooking show on You-Tube," said Sven. "I hope you will all help me."

"As long as I get to eat, then I'll help!" said Pumpkin. "As for me, I'm going to set up an unmannerly website."

"What's an unmannerly website?" asked Yolanda.

"A site about unmannerliness," replied Pumpkin. "Wait and see. What about you?"

"I'm going to build and sell Vocab Bots," said Yolanda.

Suddenly, Pumpkin whipped out his phone

and took a photo of a teen cat named Boris, who was eating a bag of chips nearby.

"Now what?" Yolanda asked.

"I spotted some unmannerliness," replied Pumpkin. "That Boris with his fake Russian accent was stuffing fifteen lime-flavored chips in his mouth at once. I think *Spotted Unmannerliness* will be a popular feature on my site."

Boris overheard what Pumpkin said, and charged toward him. "You bright orange boil! How dare you! I'm going to pound you into the ground!"

Chapter 3

The four friends took off at a run, and escaped into Cat School before Boris could catch Pumpkin.

Later that day, they met in the Science Area during after-school time.

"Would you please help me build my Vocab Bot?" Yolanda asked her friends.

"Yay!" said Pumpkin, Fritz, and Sven.

"Great. Teacher Ms. Robo Kitty gave me a robotic vacuum cleaner to use as the base of my robot," said Yolanda.

Pumpkin and Sven went to work with screwdrivers and other tools, while Yolanda and Fritz started writing a program for the robot.

After-school time was almost over. "Let's do a trial run before we go home," said Yolanda.

She pushed some buttons on the controller and the Vocab Bot started to move slowly. Then it picked up speed.

"Yowsers! Watch what you're doing!" said Pumpkin.

Yolanda tried to slow the Vocab Bot down, but it didn't respond.

The four friends watched in horror as the Vocab Bot smashed into the wall.

Crash! Bang! Boom!

Robot parts flew in all directions.

"That's quite enough for today," said Teacher Ms. Robo Kitty. "Please go home ... NOW!"

Chapter 4

Yolanda dragged her paws sadly as the cats walked to Sven's home.

"You will do better tomorrow," said Sven. "We will all help."

"In the meantime, we need to help Sven with his cooking show," said Fritz.

The friends climbed into the attic of the shed where Sven lived.

"Mistress Josheka's grandmother used to live here when it was known as a house, so we have a great kitchen," said Sven. "Thank goodness my mother is not home yet. We can cook without trouble. Pumpkin, you can record the video with your phone."

"What are you going to cook?" asked Pumpkin.

"Lutefisk," said Sven. "Please note that it is pronounced *loot a fisk*. Only complete imbeciles pronounce it *lu tee fish*."

"What in the name of the Great Cat is lutefisk?" said Pumpkin.

"It is a Viking food. You soak dried fish in lye for months," Sven replied.

"What's lye?" asked Yolanda.

"Lye is a strong solution used for cleaning," said Sven. "It is made out of ashes and water."

"Yuk," said Fritz, who usually loved fish. "What a horrible way to spoil a perfectly good fish!"

"The legend is that a group of Vikings hung their fish to dry on wooden racks. The Vikings were attacked, and their enemies burned the racks of fish. But a rainstorm blew in, putting the fire out. The leftover fish sat in a puddle of ashes and water for months. Then some hungry Vikings discovered the fish, cooked it, and ate it," said Sven. "Fortunately, I have some soaking in a pot already. Yolanda, will you please lift the lid?"

Yolanda did so, and a cloud of the worst stench she had ever smelled arose from the pot.

"Ugh," she said, choking and choking.

Sven peered over the table and asked, "Are you horking?"

Indeed, Yolanda was horking.

Pumpkin said, "Wow, I got it all on video!"

Chapter 5

Fritz's Weather Blog

Wednesday, March 15:

Weather Forecast for Josheka Farm, Laughing Thunder County, Minnesota - Mostly clear but cooler with a high of 32 degrees Fahrenheit

Fritz, Pumpkin, Sven, and Yolanda met the following morning.

"Thank the Great Cat it's teacher-in-service day, so we don't have Cat School," said Fritz. "My blimp's arrived and I need your help."

"What are we going to do?" asked Pumpkin.

"There's an ice jam on the Upper Lower River," said Fritz. "I need to make a video of it for my website."

The cats climbed aboard the blimp.

"Ready for takeoff!" said Fritz.

Up the blimp went.

"Yolanda, help me with the weather instruments. Sven, steer the blimp. Pumpkin, shoot video," said Fritz.

Soon they were over the Upper Lower River.

"Wow, look at the flooding upstream!" said Fritz. "Look at the huge chunks of ice on the river banks!"

14

The cats gazed out the windows at the sight. The ice chunks were at least eight feet tall.

"It's the Ice Age again!" said Pumpkin.

Sven was so busy looking at the ice that he forgot to steer.

Crunch! Crash! Scrape!

The cats were thrown out of their seats, but Pumpkin managed to keep his camera recording. Fritz pushed himself off the floor. He had a barometer hanging around one ear.

"By the Great Cat, what happened?" asked Fritz.

The cats peered out the windows.

"We appear to be stuck in a giant oak tree," said Yolanda.

Fritz grabbed the controls. He pushed the control stick forward. He pushed the control stick backward. He did this three times.

Finally, the blimp pulled free from the tree.

"Sven, your time as pilot is over. I'll fly us home," Fritz said.

Chapter 6

Fritz's Weather Blog

Thursday, March 16:

Weather Forecast for Josheka Farm, Laughing Thunder County, Minnesota —Clear and cold with a high of 19 degrees Fahrenheit

Pumpkin worked on his unmannerly website before going to Cat School.

"Burrrrrrrrrrrrp!"

"Pumpkin, what's that awful noise?" asked his grandmother. "I'm trying to work on my mannerly website!"

"Awwww, Grandmother, I'm just loading the Burp of the Day onto my unmannerly website," said Pumpkin.

"Pumpkin, I despair."

"But Grandmother, it's a lot of fun."

"Horrrrrrrrrrrrrrk!"

"I'm afraid to ask, but what was that?"

"Oh, that's just my latest feature – it's my Hork of the Week. It's really popular."

"That's disgusting!"

"I made a bunch of advertising money this week. I wanted to buy some candy with it, but I've been too busy with my business. So I put all of the money in my savings account to pay for college."

"But Pumpkin, I've tried very hard to teach you to be mannerly."

"Grandmother, I'm very mannerly. But sometimes it's a lot of fun to laugh at unmannerliness."

"Oh dear."

"Yeah, I just added a new feature – *Spotted Unmannerliness*."

"It sounds like a disease, Pumpkin."

"No worries, Grandmother. I got a photo of Boris stuffing fifteen lime-flavored chips into his mouth at once. He's super unmannerly!"

"Good grief, I can already hear the screams from the mothers when they see that."

"But Grandmother, I'm really helping *your* business. All those mothers will flock to your site after their young ones have visited my site. You'll probably sells zillions more of your manners training classes and books," said Pumpkin.

"But me no buts. You're still encouraging unmannerliness."

"What I'm actually encouraging is more business for you, Grandmother. In fact, I think you should pay me, as I'm increasing your sales. We'll call it a finder's fee."

"We'll call it that you're in big trouble. Get

yourself off to Cat School right now, young Pumpkin."

"Drat!" muttered Pumpkin as he left.

Chapter 7

That day, after Cat School, Yolanda took Vocab Bot 2 home for some more programming.

Her older brother, Yosh, was already home when she arrived. He was doing homework with his teen cat friends Boris, Azola, and Skoog.

"What's that?" asked Yosh, pointing a paw at Vocab Bot 2.

"It's top secret, so keep your whiskers out," said Yolanda, going into her room.

After a few minutes, a robotic voice said, "Succotash."

Yosh looked around, and then shrugged.

A short while later, a robotic voice said, "Succotash."

Yosh looked up from his homework with an annoyed look on his face.

Two minutes later, the robotic voice again said, "Succotash."

Yosh rotated his ears like a radar system, until he located the source of the sound. It was coming from Yolanda's room.

"You've got to do something about that, bro," said Boris, as he munched lime-flavored chips.

Yosh marched to Yolanda's room. "By the Great Cat, shut that stupid thing off!" he said.

At that moment, the robotic voice blasted straight at him, much louder this time, "Succotash!"

"That's it!" said Yosh, lunging toward Yolanda.

Yolanda dodged past him, running out of the house with Yosh hot on her paws.

Quickly, she ran to the shed where Sven lived.

Sven had a rope hanging from the attic window for his friends to use. Up the rope she sped.

"Hurry! Pull it up!" Yolanda said, panting.

Sven pulled the rope up just before Yosh reached it.

Yolanda caught her breath and said, "Thank you, Sven, you saved me from my beast of a brother."

Chapter 8

The friends gathered around Yolanda.

"Are you OK?" asked Fritz.

"Barely," said Yolanda. "I need a different business. This one is too dangerous. Plus, I haven't made any money yet to buy candy." She stopped and thought for a moment. "I know, I'm going to start the Tuxedo Cat Society, and I'll be the President!"

"Well, you can do that later today," said Sven. "Right now it is time to record Episode Two of my show, *New Norwegian Cooking*."

"What's cooking today?" Pumpkin asked. He laughed as he got out his phone.

"You wanted me to cook something with your favorite food, the gizzard of a lizard. So today, I am making Gizzard Lefse," said Sven. "Pumpkin, start recording."

Pumpkin held up his phone and touched the screen.

"On *New Norwegian Cooking*," said Sven, looking into the camera, "we like to give the old classics a fresh twist. First, my assistant Yolanda will place upon the table the lefse that I just made. For those of you who do not know, lefse is sort of a Norwegian tortilla, made out of mashed potatoes, butter, cream, and sugar. Please note that it is pronounced *lef sa*. Only idiotic fools say *left see*."

Yolanda placed the lefse on the table.

"Instead of butter, we will put a spread of lizard gizzard on this fine piece of lefse," said Sven. "Luckily, I have already prepared the gizzard. Yolanda, please spread the gizzard on the lefse." He pointed at it with his paw.

Yolanda grabbed a spoon and went over to the bowl. It contained a foul slime of brown lumps. The smell was something awful! She started choking and choking.

"Are you horking?" Sven asked as he peered over the table at her.

"That's a wrap," said Pumpkin from behind his phone.

Chapter 9

Fritz's Weather Blog

Friday, March 17: Weather Forecast for Joshe-ka Farm, Laughing Thunder County, Minnesota - Partly cloudy with a high of 32 degrees Fahrenheit

After Cat School, the four met to walk together to their homes.

"This weather is totally and completely boring," said Fritz. "I'm going to seed the clouds to get some action for my weather blog. I need *extreme* weather to attract viewers and advertisers, if I'm ever going to make enough money to buy candy. Will you please help me?"

"What is cloud seeding?" asked Sven.

"You drop a special dust high in the sky, and

water clings to the tiny particles, making clouds," Fritz replied.

"I'm in! I'm in!" said Pumpkin.

"I'm in! I'm in!" said Yolanda.

"I am in!" said Sven.

The friends ran to the blimp. Soon they were floating over a formation of puffy white clouds that looked like cotton balls.

"Those are cumulous clouds," explained Fritz. "Pumpkin, keep the video running. Yolanda, open the hatch. Sven, push out the cloud-seeding crystals."

Each cat did his or her part.

Soon, the friends heard the rumble of thunder.

"Great. It worked!" said Fritz. "I'm going to bring the blimp in for landing now."

As the blimp descended through the clouds, the wind tossed it this way and that. Everyone except Fritz began to turn green.

Then it began to snow – big, wet flakes of snow. Fritz peered through the snow, searching for the landing pad.

The thunder boomed again.

"Oh wow, thundersnow," said Fritz. "That's so cool!"

"Just land this thing," moaned Sven.

Finally, Fritz brought the blimp down with a bump.

As the friends staggered out, they saw some very angry cats returning from hunting.

"It's amazing," said Sven's mother. "My gopher dug in deep after all that racket. It's no use hunting now!"

"I can't believe this thundersnow!" said Pumpkin's grandmother. Ice crystals were forming on her whiskers.

"I'm miserable," grumbled Yosh, shaking his wet fur like a dog.

The thunder boomed again.

"One minute it was fine, then thundersnow," said Fritz's uncle as he brushed wet snow off his head with a paw. "If you ask me, it's not natural."

The four friends looked at each other with worry, then they slunk into the bushes to hide until the older cats went by.

Chapter 10

Fritz's Weather Blog

Saturday, March 18: Weather Forecast for Josheka Farm, Laughing Thunder County, Minnesota – Sunny and warm with a high of 50 degrees Fahrenheit

Yolanda woke up early to hang a banner from the windmill.

Sven ran up to her as she was working.

"Guess what?" he said, hopping around. "A TV crew from Minneapolis is coming here tomorrow to do a news segment about my next episode!"

"Awesome!" Yolanda gave him a high paw. "That's great news! But for now, would you please help me with this banner?"

"*Tuxedo Cat Society*," Sven read. "Why are you hanging that banner up?"

"Today's the first meeting," said Yolanda. "I've made a lot of money on membership fees. I can't wait to buy some candy!"

As the two finished hanging the banner, tuxedo cats of every shape and size began streaming up the driveway to the windmill.

"As President of TCS, the Tuxedo Cat Society, I welcome you one and all!" said Yolanda. "Please step up and buy your tickets. Activity booths are to your left. I hope you enjoy the first meeting of the TCS!"

At noon, Fritz and Pumpkin left their booths and checked in with Yolanda.

"Way more cats came than I expected, so I'm

running out of activities and supplies. I don't know what to do!" she said with a tired sigh.

"I can sing," said Fritz. "I'll entertain them with some of my songs."

He jumped onto a hay bale, and started singing one of the songs from his weather blog: "*It's an Arctic Inversion.*"

"More!" cheered the mass of tuxedo cats.

Fritz then sang another song from his weather blog. It was called, "*Beware of the Moray Eel.*"

He sang more and more songs. He sang until his throat was sore.

Still the tuxedo cats yelled for more.

Chapter 11

Fritz couldn't sing any more. He jumped down from the hay bale and headed to the milk dish to soothe his sore throat.

The tuxedo cats continued to yell for more.

Yolanda was worried. "What am I going to do?" she asked Pumpkin and Sven.

"No worries. I'll handle this," said Pumpkin.

He ran to his booth and came back with a bag. Then he jumped onto the hay bale.

The tuxedo cats continued to yell for more.

"Now it's time to enter the Great Burp App Giveaway!" said Pumpkin. "Step right up and buy a ticket for the Giveaway! Multiple prizes! Many winners!"

Tuxedo cats mobbed Pumpkin. Soon his

bright orange fur was lost from view among the mass of black and white.

"Now for the drawing," said Pumpkin, pushing the mob of cats back from his bag of tickets.

"You there," he said, pointing his paw at a small tuxedo cat who was being crushed by the bigger cats. "You can draw the tickets. The rest of you – stand back!"

The small cat jumped about with excitement. This was the greatest thing that had ever happened to her!

"Draw out five tickets and hand them to me," said Pumpkin.

The small cat did as she was told.

"Now read out the numbers," said Pumpkin.

"Twenty-seven, ninety-eight, forty-six, seventy-three, and fifteen," said the small cat with pride.

"Holders of those tickets, meet at the Unmannerly Booth to pick up your prizes," said Pumpkin. "You too, little one. You get a prize for helping."

The tuxedo cats swarmed over to Pumpkin's booth.

"All winners receive a free copy of my Burp App to install on their phones," announced Pumpkin.

Soon, the sounds of burps echoed throughout Josheka Farm.

"By the Great Cat, that's disgusting. It sounds like a chorus of frogs," said Pumpkin's grandmother.

Chapter 12

Fritz's Weather Blog

Sunday, March 19: Weather Forecast for Josheka Farm, Laughing Thunder County, Minnesota – Overcast and cool, with a high of 32 degrees Fahrenheit

The four cats met the TV crew in Sven's attic kitchen.

"Did you know your cooking show has gone viral on YouTube?" said the reporter, sticking a microphone in Sven's face.

"I had no idea!" said Sven. "I have been too busy inventing new dishes to check on such things."

"Your show has had over one million views," said the reporter.

Sven's eyes almost popped out of his head.

"We want to film you in action," said the reporter.

The TV cameraman and Pumpkin started filming.

"Today on *New Norwegian Cooking*, I am making a famous Norwegian cookie, the krumkake," said Sven. "Please note that it is pronounced *kroom kaka*. It is offensive to call it a crumb cake as so many ignoramuses do. You make the cookie on this special iron, which is somewhat like a thin waffle iron. When the krumkake is fresh off the iron, I will shape it. My assistant Yolanda will pour the batter." He waved a paw towards Yolanda.

"Meanwhile, I will start whipping the cream, vanilla, and sugar for the filling. Ah, notice the cone-like shape of the krumkake? It is perfect for holding fillings. I have placed my whipped cream into this icing cone and will now squirt the mixture into the krumkake. Yolanda, please hold one of the krumkake for me."

Yolanda held a krumkake in her paws.

Sven squeezed a bit of whipped cream onto his paw and tasted it. "Perfect. We are ready. Yolanda, in return for all your help, you deserve a taste as well. Please open your mouth for a small squirt of this delightful whipped cream."

Yolanda opened her little pink mouth.

But Sven's paw slipped, and a huge blob of whipped cream shot down Yolanda's throat.

Yolanda began choking! She choked and choked.

"Are you horking?" asked Sven.

"That's a wrap!" said Pumpkin.

The TV crew cheered.

"Maybe you should re-name this the "*Are You Horking Show*," said the reporter, laughing. "Anyway, we're very sorry that one of you is ill, but as a small token of our thanks we've brought a box of candy for all of you."

"Finally, we get some candy!" said Pumpkin as he pumped an orange paw in the air.

About the Author

S. S. Curtis grew up on a farm shared with a peak population of fifty-four cats of every color, shape, size, and personality imaginable. Her child continued the cat tradition, but with a twist – the population expanded to include both living cats and toy cats. All of those cats are her inspiration for the Cats of Laughing Thunder. You can explore the world of the Laughing Thunder Cats at

www.laughingthunder.com.